PETER'S PIXIE

DONN KUSHNER • *Illustrated by* SYLVIE DAIGNEAULT

Introduction by TONY KUSHNER

TUNDRA BOOKS

To my grandsons Noah and Wesley.

D. K.

———

To wonderful Rachel and to the memory of Donn,
the remarkable man whose words inspired me.

S. D.

Published in Canada by Tundra Books,
481 University Avenue, Toronto, Ontario M5G 2E9

Published in the United States by Tundra Books of Northern New York,
P.O. Box 1030, Plattsburgh, New York 12901

Library of Congress Control Number: 2003100905

National Library of Canada Cataloguing in Publication

Kushner, Donn, 1927-2001
Peter's pixie / Donn Kushner ; illustrated by Sylvie Daigneault.

ISBN 0-88776-603-X

I. Daigneault, Sylvie II. Title.

PS8571.U82P48 2003   jC813'.54   C2003-900693-X
                            PZ7

We acknowledge the financial support of the Government of Canada through the Book Publishing
Industry Development Program and that of the Government of Ontario through the Ontario Media
Development Corporation's Ontario Book Initiative. We further acknowledge the support of the Canada
Council for the Arts and the Ontario Arts Council for our publishing program.

Design by K.T. Njo
Printed and bound in Hong Kong, China

1 2 3 4 5 6   08 07 06 05 04 03

INTRODUCTION

by Tony Kushner

Donn Kushner was a tall, thin microbiologist with glasses who spent a lot of time thinking about small things: microbes, pixies, children. He was a gentle person, although he had a temper, and he found the world amusing, though it worried him as well. He was enormously generous, eager to make friends, endlessly curious about other people. At the same time, he was quite shy; he hid his shyness behind jokes, behind formidable learning, behind the stories he loved to tell.

He didn't have an easy childhood. He grew up in the United States during the Great Depression, Jewish in a small Southern town. His parents were kind and loving people, but burdened by shyness themselves. Donn grew up feeling uncertain about the world's affection. About his affection for the world there was never any doubt. He built a rich and beautiful life for himself; he was a scholar, a teacher, a husband, a father, a grandfather. He traveled every-where, enjoying the adventure, intrigued by the strange landscapes and cities he encountered, but much more interested in the people he met.

For all his traveling, his professional accomplishments, his great love of literature and music – he played the violin – it was always easy to see the bookish, lonely boy Donn had been who grew into a lovable, fascinating, uncomfortable adult.

I think his decision to write for children arrived with the first of his grandsons. Like most gifted authors for children, he understood two important things: children are interested in the same things as adults, although their perspectives are different; and children's literature can address any topic, express any ambiguity, once the appropriate tone has been found. Like most storytellers, Donn wrote for the children at hand and for the child he once was.

Donn died in 2001. His family misses him, of course, as do his many friends. It's lovely to have his stories to enjoy, to help us think about him and remember. We hope, and we know Donn hopes, that you too will enjoy his stories – especially the one you are about to read. Like much of Donn's work, it contains a quiet imperative: pay attention to small things.

Peter's family called the old lady next door Aunt Agnes, for that was her name. She grew herbs in her garden and told Peter all about the small magic people – elves, who dwell in the forests; gnomes, who lurk underground; leprechauns, who hide pots of gold; and pixies, who sometimes steal into houses.

"Pixies are mischievous," she said, "but very good companions."

Peter saw his own pixie on the day that his new ball went astray. He'd been throwing it at the net fixed to the big oak tree. A small hand darted out of the branches and batted the ball right into a bowl of salad.

Peter heard a tiny giggle, which might have been the wind in the trees, and looked up. A sharp little face with bright blue eyes looked right at him and winked. The face's owner wore clothes just the color of the leaves. It looked very young and very old at the same time. Peter knew it must be a pixie.

"Oh, Peter!" his mother said. "There's salad everywhere."

His father said, "It was an accident."

"But he has to be more responsible," said his mother. "He's going to be a big brother soon."

That afternoon, his parents brought out the cradle Peter had used when he was very small. His mother painted it white and gold and lined its head and foot with a cloth full of stars. She folded the blanket Aunt Agnes had made and carefully laid it in the cradle. "Look how lovely, Peter," she said. "I must show your father."

Peter peered into the cradle. The pixie crawled out from under the blanket and set to rocking, side to side. Peter heard his parents' footsteps behind him and turned around. The cradle was still rocking when he looked at it again, but it was empty.

"You're too old for the cradle now, Peter," said his mother. "That's for the new baby."

His father put a new wheel on the tiny wagon Peter used to pull. He dusted and washed Peter's old blocks. Aunt Agnes was called to come and admire the toys. "What a lucky baby this will be! Shall we have a cup of tea, dear?" she said to Peter's mother.

"We'll be in the kitchen, Peter. Don't touch the clean toys," said his mother.

As soon as they were gone, the pixie appeared. It fell to work making a stack of the blocks, almost to the ceiling.

"Peter, come and join us for milk and cookies," called his mother.

CRASH! The blocks were scattered on the floor.

"I declare, Peter, you've gone back to being a baby!"

Peter said nothing. He did not think he could explain about the pixie.

Before the baby was born, Peter's mother's friends gave a party. They brought pajamas and shirts and rattles and stuffed animals. Peter looked at these little baby things and thought that this would leave the old toys for the pixie and him to play with. Then he saw the pixie itself sitting among the gifts, not moving at all.

As the ladies were leaving they said, "What a wonderful doll! Who brought it? Did you? Did you?"

Peter's mother was too busy saying good-bye to look. And when the ladies had gone, the pixie had disappeared too. Peter felt lonely and wished the pixie had stayed. For even with all his pranks, Peter really liked him.

Peter went next door to ask Aunt Agnes about pixies. "Once they come, do they always stay?"

She shook her head. "You have to give them gifts."

"What kind of gifts?"

"Some like bowls of milk. Some like coins. Some like a dish of water to wash in. Some like something else."

Peter put out a bowl of milk...

. . . but the cat drank it.

He put out some coins on the kitchen floor . . .

. . . but his mother saw them and put them in the coin jar.

He put out a big pot of water . . .

. . . but his father overturned it.

"Be more careful," his mother said. "Give the cat her water in the regular dish."
    The pixie only glanced at these gifts, turned up its sharp little nose, and walked away.

When the time came for Peter's mother to have the baby, Aunt Agnes gave her a pot of basil and rosemary for the hospital room and settled into the house to take care of Peter.

"Did your pixie like the gifts?" she asked.

Peter could not say. He had searched and searched but had seen no sign of the pixie.

In the morning Aunt Agnes said, "Come see your new baby brother."

"He's a real little elf," Peter's father said proudly.

"He's a regular pixie!" Peter's mother said.

Aunt Agnes nodded. "He'll be a new playmate for you. Think of all you have to teach him!"

Peter's mother held the new baby in her arms. He wasn't crying. Peter looked at the baby. A sharp little face with bright blue eyes looked back at him and winked.